MW00760934

SAFE

ANGIE THOMPSON

Quiet Waters Press

Lynchburg, Virginia

ISBN: 978-1-951001-06-3 (pbk)
ISBN: 978-1-951001-05-6 (ePub)

For Tim, just because

Thanks to everyone who helped inspire this story, who read and loved on it with me, and who helped me brainstorm when I was totally stuck for a title. And special thanks to Rebekah for coming up with the winner!

SAFE

"How's he doing, Mama?"

I took the steps to the porch at a trot, letting the ends of my scarf trail behind me in the wind as I scanned Mom's face. Little lines I didn't remember seeing before were etched into her forehead.

"He's been a little better, Mads. Much better than the last time you saw him."

"Oh, that's good. You know I didn't want to go but—"

"No, no, sweetheart." Mom held the door open and motioned me inside. "You had exams. We've been fine. Lots of church ladies bringing casseroles. And Pastor Gene says they've got men lined up to cover the lawn and sidewalk until Bryson's back on his feet."

"They're good people." I swallowed a lump in my throat as I tossed my coat and scarf onto a chair.

"Don't I know it." The gratitude in Mom's tone was real, but there was something else behind it, a worry she hadn't put into words.

"What are the doctors saying?"

"He's doing well, all things considered. Won't be walking for a while, but they've got him off the heavy painkillers and down to double-strength regular stuff. And he's home now, so that's a big step. He's resting a lot. Catching up on some shows and some reading."

"Mama, what aren't you telling me?" I bent down a little to look her straight in the eyes, and she winced and looked away.

"It's nothing, Mads. Nothing really. I've just been thinking—maybe I ought to cancel this trip."

"Cancel your Christmas splurge with Aunt Jenny? Mom, why? If Bryson's okay—" My heartbeat picked up suddenly.

"He's not, is he? There's more you're not telling me."

"No, Maddy, no." Mom gripped my hand and held it tight. "He's okay, really." She put a little too much emphasis on the last word, like maybe she was trying to convince herself as well as me.

"Then why are you worrying? You've trusted us to take care of each other before. And this trip is important to you. It's got to be serious if you're thinking of staying home."

"I don't know, Mads, it's just—" Mom bit her lips together. "He's so quiet. Almost—I don't know—guarded. It's not like Bryse."

"Ah. Okay." I tried to let out my relieved sigh a little at a time so Mom wouldn't notice it. Quiet. Guarded. Hiding his pain. That was more like Bryse than she knew, especially after Dad died, except he must be too spent to realize he wasn't doing it well. "That's probably normal with everything he's been through, don't you think?"

"Probably." The worry lines near her eyes didn't fade. I put an arm around her shoulders.

"Bryse'll be fine, Mom. He just needs a little time. How's he sleeping at night? You know he doesn't function well on low sleep."

"He's only had to call me for a pain pill once or twice. Says it's hard to get to sleep sometimes, but otherwise he says he's doing fine."

"Have you asked him about canceling?"

"I mentioned that I was thinking about it."

"And what did he say?"

"Said I should go, of course. But—I don't know, honey—I can just tell when one of my babies needs their mama."

Bryson must be seriously off his game to make Mom feel like that. Either that or he was hurt worse than he was letting on. I squeezed her shoulders hard.

"You haven't canceled anything yet, have you?"

Mom shook her head, but I could tell she was about a second away from making the calls.

"Let me talk to Bryse. Find out what he really wants. You know a couple days of Madison time could be just the thing he needs."

"You always were good for him." Mom's smile was a little teary. I turned toward the stairs, but she stopped me. "He's in the parlor, Mads. Didn't want me to have to climb the stairs all day."

So he was home but not fully settled back in. That could have a lot to do with the tension Mom was sensing. I took the hallway to the little back room that stubbornly refused to be a family room or a den or anything other than the old-fashioned parlor we'd christened it when we first moved in. At the door, I knocked softly and poked my head in.

"Hey, I'm the new nurse. Looking for the orthopedic ward."

"Maddy." A smile slid across Bryson's face. He reached for the remote and muted the TV, then held out his arms to me. I eased

5

down onto the side of the bed, and we held each other for a long minute.

My mind played back over the scenes Mom had described—the semi crowding his lane on a tight turn, his little truck smashed against the mountain, the firefighters prying his legs free with the jaws of life. The realization that I'd almost lost my brother flooded me again, mixed with a fervent prayer of thanks that I hadn't. When his grip loosened, I let go and pulled back, and Bryson sank against the pillows and squinted up at me.

"How'd your exams go?"

"Not too bad, considering all I could think about was getting back home to you."

"Mads." The accident hadn't damaged his scolding big-brother tone. I smiled.

"I did fine, Bryse. At least, I think I did. Won't have the results for a couple weeks yet. Looks like you're moving up in the world, though. Ground floor suite. Private TV. Room service." I nodded toward the dishes sitting on the little table next to his bed, and he rolled his eyes. The response was typical Bryse, but the tired, almost languid air was new.

I glanced around the room, smiling to myself at the half-transformation Bryson's temporary residence had made. Black and white geometric headboard against solid oak bookcases. Flat-screen TV on top of the old upright piano. Laptop and charging cables sharing shelf space with antique hardbacks.

"Love what you've done with the place, by the way."

He swatted at my arm, not as forcefully as he would have a few weeks ago, but his lips relaxed into a smile. I reached for his hand and gripped it hard.

"I need you to be completely honest with me, Bryse. Just for a second. Mom's thinking of canceling her trip. Any reason you want or need her here now that I'm around?"

Bryson hesitated, and I caught the almost imperceptible movement of his teeth against his lip, but in the next instant, he shook his head.

"No, she should definitely go. She won't get to see Aunt Jen for another year. Tell her

7

if she doesn't go, I'll lock her out of the room and make you take care of me anyway, so she'd better do it."

The words were right, but the tone was off, laced with a hint of uncertainty that was hard to describe. I'd never heard him pretend cheerfulness so badly. No wonder Mom wanted to stay.

"You're sure?" I studied his face carefully, and he gave me a small grin.

"I'm sure. You can tell her I'll be fine, unless you plan to go off gallivanting and leave me on my own here." A bit of the usual sparkle glinted in his eye, highlighting his unusual vulnerability and making me hope that a few days of banter and fun would bring back more of the brother I loved. I narrowed my eyes at him.

"I do not gallivant."

"Lindsay Olson." He held up two fingers, and I scowled.

"Those don't count."

"Since when?"

"Since you were supposed to be watching me, not the other way around."

"Uh-huh." Bryson arched his eyebrows, and I stuck out my tongue.

"You're one to talk. Try Ninja Fury 5."

"House of mirrors."

"Carnival popcorn."

"Ice cream earrings."

"You two okay?" Mom popped her head in the door, looking a bit concerned, and I laughed.

"Just naming all the times one of us has left the other behind. Bryson seems to think I'll run off and leave him here, but I'm just relieved I won't have to keep my eye on him every second."

Bryson's grin was more relaxed than it'd been since I came in, and Mom's eyes softened as she walked over to the bed and stroked his hair.

"Good to have her home, isn't it, Bryse?"

"Yeah. Home where I can keep an eye on her. Speaking of which—boys, Madison. I want names."

"What boys?" I gave him a puzzled look, and he narrowed his eyes.

"Any boys you met this semester. Just because you're away at college doesn't mean I lose vetting privileges."

"For Pete's sake, Bryson!" I threw up my hands with my best exasperated tone. "You already know Josh and Locke and Petey. And you met Petey's friend Aaron over the summer. There's no other guys I hang out with."

"I've heard you've been unavailable for several get-togethers this fall."

"Because I've been studying. Senior classes are a lot harder."

"And you've been seen walking with a boy near the library on more than one occasion."

My eyes narrowed as I tried to decide which of my friends deserved pummeling when I got back to campus. Locke probably, since he was most likely to use the cut-through by the library on the way to biology lab.

"It was a group project, and we both happened to be free right after class. What was I supposed to do, run ahead of him?"

"Name?" Bryson pressed, and I sighed.

10

"Kensley Henderson. He's a poli-sci major, so our classes overlap."

"You've met him before?"

"He's been in a couple of my classes. I might have spoken to him in the hall once or twice."

"So why haven't I heard of him?"

"Bryson, honestly! Why don't you just download my class rosters and 'vet' every boy on them? Better yet, call the registrar and get a full enrollment list. This is ridiculous." I glanced up at Mom, who was leaning against Bryson's headboard, all the worry lines on her face smoothed away in her smile. "Tell you what, Mom. I'll go shopping with Aunt Jenny this year. Her third degree isn't half as bad as Bryson's."

"Sounds like the two of you are going to be okay here without me." Mom leaned over and kissed Bryson's forehead. His smile slipped for a fraction of a second, but it was back in place before Mom could notice.

"Sure we are. You have a great time. And tell Aunt Jen five fractures better net me more than a baseball cap this year."

11

Mom hesitated, and I understood why. That vague something—vulnerability?—was back in his tone, undercutting his cheerful words in a way it hadn't when he'd been pestering me. I squeezed Mom's arm.

"Yes, go. Good presents trump a nosy brother every time. Right, Bryse?"

"Absolutely."

"Glad you're finally admitting you're nosy." I gave him a triumphant smirk, and he swatted my arm again.

"Brat."

"Tyrant."

We grinned at each other, and Mom chuckled.

"I'll get my bags."

After helping Mom finish packing and get out the door and lugging my own bags into the house, I pulled out my tablet and settled in the chair closest to Bryson's bed. I had intended to read, but instead I found myself scrutinizing my brother. The TV was on, but he gave no sign that he was doing more than mindlessly staring at it. His eyes blinked heavily several times like he was ready to fall asleep, but each time he roused himself, blinking hard and repositioning slightly as though to keep himself awake. A nap would probably be good for him; the dark circles under his eyes said he hadn't been sleeping well, no matter what he'd told Mom.

Finally, I leaned over and touched his arm, and his eyes jumped to my face.

"Are you watching this?" I nodded toward the TV, and he shrugged.

"Seen one home improvement show, you've seen 'em all."

Definitely time to turn it off. I reached for the remote.

"Want to do something together?"

"Sure. What'd you have in mind?" Bryson looked mildly interested, and he didn't protest when I turned the TV off.

"Want me to read to you?"

My reading always put Bryson to sleep faster than anything else. It was a bit of a dubious honor, but I was willing to waive the point if it would help him rest.

Something I couldn't interpret flashed in Bryson's eyes, and he winced.

"Maybe another time, Mads? I'm—kinda storied out right now."

"I could play." I glanced at the piano, and he bit his lip.

"How about a game?"

Not exactly what I'd been going for, but anything had to be better for him than lying there watching TV like a lump. I nodded.

"What'd you have in mind?"

"Anything."

"So, Twister?"

"Oh, that's cold!" Bryson groaned, and I grinned.

"I guess that means charades is out, too."

"Just go find something, knucklehead." A genuine smile flashed beneath his tired eyes. I decided priority one would be helping him relax; priority two would be getting him to rest.

14

When I returned with a stack of options, Bryson chose a trivia game, and I cleared the dishes off his table and swung it over the bed. It felt just like old times, reading the questions in goofy voices, making wild guesses for answers we didn't know, and trying to squeeze in an extra space or two when our opponent wasn't looking. Or it would have if not for the little distracted lapses that Bryson sometimes sank into and the dull, hollow look in his eyes before he snapped out of them.

I finally declared victory, and in my celebration, accidentally-purposely sent the game pieces flying so I'd have to chase after them. There was nothing fake about my heavy breathing when I shut the lid and settled down next to Bryson's bed again.

"Okay, I could go for a rest. I'm beat. How about you?"

"I've been resting all day." Bryson gave a half-laugh that didn't hold any humor. "But go ahead if you want to." His hand reached for the remote, and I stopped it.

15

"I'm not really that tired. I thought you might be. Sleep's supposed to be good for healing, you know."

That undefinable something flashed in Bryson's eyes again, and when he answered, it was with the forced lightness that had worried Mom so much.

"Have to get myself good and worn out today so I'll sleep tonight. Don't worry about me, Mads. I'll be fine."

Everything about this felt off, but pushing him would only make him work harder to cover it up. I squeezed his hand instead.

"You want to play something else?"

"If you're not too tired."

I shook my head and pulled a checkerboard from the pile. We were in the middle of our third round when I glanced at the clock and realized it was past suppertime. I excused myself to the kitchen and made a quick phone call. When I returned, Bryson gave me a quizzical half-smile.

"What's the casserole of the night?"

"Nothing."

"Come again?"

16

"I figured you had to be pretty sick of casseroles by now. So I ordered pizza."

"Maddy, you're an angel!" Bryson pressed his hand to his heart with such a rapturous look that I laughed. "Sausage and mushroom?"

"I happen to know my brother pretty well." I grinned over at him. To my surprise, Bryson blinked hard, and his smile dimmed a little.

"Yeah, you do. Thanks, Mads."

I hadn't imagined such a little thing would touch him so deeply. I reached over and brushed back a strand of hair that had fallen over his eyes.

"Getting a little long, isn't it?"

I was totally unprepared for the pain that suddenly etched his face or the alarming pallor that came with it. He drew in a long, shuddering breath, and I gripped his shoulder.

"Bryse? Are you okay? Talk to me. Is it your legs?"

He shook his head with an effort.

"Something I did? Something I said?"

17

Bryson squeezed his eyes shut, and I tightened my grip.

"Bryse, talk to me!"

"It's—nothing, Maddy." I could see him struggling to control his breathing. "I'm—okay."

"Bryse, please tell me. If I said something—"

"You didn't." He shook his head, pulling in a deep lungful of air. "Yeah, it's—getting long. I had an appointment—that afternoon."

That afternoon. The day of the accident.

"Oh, Bryse."

"It's okay. The silliest things—remind me sometimes." His breathing was easing a little, and I could feel his shoulder starting to relax under my hand.

"Not silly at all." I took a deep breath. "Tell you what. I'll cut it for you one of these days. Then it won't get in your way, and you won't have to think about it."

"Madison, you wouldn't!" Bryson's eyes opened wide, and he shifted away from my hand.

"I have cut hair before, you know."

18

"Not on your life! No way are you touching mine! Bring one pair of scissors into this room, and I'm calling Mom back."

"Touchy!" I teased.

"Promise me, Madison!" The horror on his face was ten times better than the pinched look it'd worn when I'd dredged up memories of the accident, but I decided not to press the point. No use getting him keyed up for no reason when what he needed was sleep.

"Okay, Bryse. I won't touch it. Promise."

He slumped back down against the pillows, and I gently tucked a few sweaty strands behind his ear.

"Touching it." Bryse opened one eye in a mischievous squint, and I smiled.

"Guilty as charged. I promise I won't cut it. But I can help you wash it tomorrow, if you want."

"That would be awesome." He opened both eyes and gave me a wobbly but genuine smile. "Thanks, Mads."

"Love you, Bryse." I rubbed my knuckles lightly over his cheek, then straightened as the doorbell rang. "And I have the pizza to prove it."

A bit of color had come back into Bryson's cheeks by the time we'd finished the pizza and he'd grilled me about classes, boys, career prospects, teachers, boys, how much stuff he'd need to help me move home, and more boys. Toward the end of my third repetition of more nothing, his eyes started to close, and I wondered if the fading adrenaline would be his ally tonight in helping him get to sleep. After a long interval where I began to think he'd actually dropped off, he opened his eyes, shook his head, and squinted up at me.

"You gotta be pretty beat, Mads. All those hours driving, and you got an early start."

That was projection if I'd ever heard it. I smiled and shook my head.

"I'll head up after you fall asleep."

Bryson swallowed hard.

20

"I'll be there in about ten seconds. Go on, Mads, please? I'll feel better if I know you're not sitting up."

Something in me protested at the thought, but if it was what it took to get him to rest... I stood up and gently grazed his cheek with my knuckles.

"Where's Mom been sleeping?"

"Her room. Why?" His words were starting to slur.

That didn't make any sense. Her room was farther from the parlor than mine was.

"Can she hear you from there?"

"Hmm?"

"Bryse." As much as I didn't want to, I shook his shoulder a little, and he jerked fully awake.

"What?" His breath caught for a second, and he looked a little disoriented until his eyes focused on my face. "What's wrong?"

"How does Mom hear you if you need her at night?"

"Oh." He let out his breath in a rush and reached for something next to his pillow.

"Radios. She left hers in your room. Don't worry; I'll pester you if I need you."

Something was wrong with this picture. A radio required Bryse to be awake and aware in order to alert anyone. What if the medicine wore off while he was asleep? There was no way I could hear him moaning or tossing from all the way upstairs.

"I'm surprised she didn't go with a baby monitor."

Bryson laughed, but there was an odd, almost desperate note to it.

"She thought about it. I'm the one who suggested the radios. You know how I talk in my sleep sometimes. No reason to keep you awake listening to me mumble about french fry invasions."

He was trying to make me smile at the memory, and I obliged, but I felt more unsettled than ever. Bryson was long over the embarrassment of being a sleep talker, and Mom would be more than willing to lose a little rest to make sure he was okay. Why had he pushed for the radios? Was it just his unnecessary protectiveness? That fit with Bryson, but my gut screamed that there was more.

"I'll call, Mads. Don't worry." His eyes were closing again, but he squinted up at me as though begging me to believe him.

"Night, Bryse." I kissed one finger and touched it to his forehead, then quietly turned out the light and left the room.

My heart pounded as I ran up the stairs, flung open my door, and scooped up the radio. I sat down on my bed and stared at it as I tried to put the fear clawing at my stomach into words.

Bryson had promised to call when he needed me. Which meant he'd call when he admitted he needed me. Which probably meant he'd wait until the pain was too bad for him to fight through on his own. Bryson was nothing if not stubborn. And protective. But so was I. And I was not going to leave my brother to fight his pain alone until he thought it was worth waking me up.

I rummaged through the hall closet until I found an air mattress and quickly hooked up the pump, relying on the fact that if I couldn't hear Bryson from upstairs, he couldn't hear me from the parlor. When it was ready, I maneuvered it down the stairs and into the hallway as quietly as I could, thankful for once that Bryson wasn't able to leave his bed and stumble over me in the night. I settled my bedding on top of it and the radio nearby, feeling much more peaceful now that I would hear my brother if he really needed me, whether he thought he did or not.

It was still early, so I pulled out my tablet and settled down to read for a while before bed. I had just laid it down and was preparing to slip under the covers when a noise from Bryson's room stopped me. I waited and listened, and the noise came again. Not a moan of pain, but a cry of fear. I sprang to my feet and burst through the door. Flipping on the light, I saw my brother writhing on the bed, eyes closed, breathing heavy, sweat pouring down his face.

"Bryse!" I gripped his arms and felt them shaking. It had to be a dream. "Bryse!" I shook him hard.

24

His eyes flew open, and he sat up straight, gasping for breath and clutching desperately at his chest. I slid onto the bed behind him and wrapped my arms around his shoulders.

"Just breathe, Bryse. Just breathe. It's okay."

He was trembling now, more violently than he had in his sleep. I pulled him tighter as he fought for breath.

"Bryse, it's okay. You're safe."

"I—I can't stop it." The pain was laced with a panic I'd never heard in my brother's voice. He gulped more air and tried to turn to look at me. "I'm sorry—"

"It's okay. It's okay. Just breathe." I laid my head on his shoulder and tried to steady my own breathing for him to follow. "You don't have to be sorry for anything. I've got you. Shhh."

Ever so slowly, Bryson's breathing eased, and his trembling subsided to occasional shudders. Something wet splashed my hand, and I realized with a start that he was crying.

"Bryse, it's all right." My own voice cracked as I rubbed my cheek against his shoulder. "You're going to be okay."

"I hate that you're seeing me like this." The words came out in a broken whisper, and I rubbed my hands gently down his arms.

"How long, Bryse?"

"How long what?" He was back to playing stubborn. That was probably a good sign. But he wasn't getting away with it this time.

"How long have you been having these? Nightmares. Panic attacks. Whatever they are. This wasn't your first one." I didn't leave room for him to deny it. Bryson drew a shuddering breath and didn't answer. "Since you came home from the hospital?"

A second's pause, then a barely perceptible nod.

"And before that?"

Another nod, even fainter.

"You haven't told Mom."

The tiniest of head shakes.

"How often do they come?"

The silence stretched for a long moment before he answered in a voice so low I almost missed it.

"Every time I fall asleep."

It all made sense now. His refusal to nap during the day. The way he'd sent me to bed when he couldn't keep his eyes open. His insistence on a radio instead of a monitor.

"Bryson, why didn't you tell someone?"

"Tell them what?" His breathing started to speed up again. "That I can't get a grip? That every time I close my eyes, I'm staring down the grille of a semi? That I start randomly sweating and shaking for no good reason?" He lifted trembling fingers to prove his point, and I sprang from my spot and settled next to him, gripping his hands tightly in my own.

"No good reason? Bryse, you were in an accident. You could have died. This isn't about getting a grip. This is normal. People respond to trauma this way all the time. It's not about powering through. It's about letting your body and brain have time to process what happened. It'll fade, honest. But you've got to stop pushing yourself. You've got to stop shutting us out. You've let me lean on you about a million times. It's time to let yourself lean on me for once."

When Bryson didn't answer, I leaned over and rested my cheek against his clammy one. Another shiver coursed through him, this one feeling more like cold than fear. I eased him back down to the pillows, and he didn't resist. After tucking the comforter carefully around him, I hurried to the kitchen and came back with a damp cloth and a mug of warm strawberry milk. I wiped the lingering traces of sweat and tears from his forehead and cheeks, then lifted his head and held the milk to his lips. After the first sip, Bryson gasped and drew in a deep breath, then eagerly reached for the mug. I pulled it away.

"Slow sips, Bryse. Don't gulp it."

I held the mug to his lips again, and he drank as fast as I let him. When the milk was gone, he fell back on the pillows with a sigh that seemed to mingle contentment and weariness. I tucked the covers around him again and stroked the damp, too long hair back from his forehead.

"Try to sleep, Bryse. Maybe the dreams won't come this time."

"They will." His eyes clouded, and he swallowed hard.

"Maybe they will. But I'll be here. Next time. And the next time. And the time after that. And we'll beat them. Together."

"Maddy?" There was a hint of a tremor in his voice. "I'm sorry."

"Don't—" I started, but he shook his head.

"I'm sorry I—I didn't want you to stay with me." A pang of hurt stabbed, but before it had time to settle, he continued. "You know me—too well. I was afraid you'd—find out."

"Oh, Bryse." Tears sprang to my eyes, and I brushed his cheek with my knuckles.

"I was wrong, Mads. I need you. I've missed you so bad."

I gave up trying to blink back the tears as I leaned over and kissed his forehead.

"I'm here, Bryse. I'm here for you. Whatever you need. As long as it takes. And

Mom's here, too. She can handle a lot more than we give her credit for sometimes. God never meant you to go through this alone."

Bryson's head dipped in what might have been a nod, then rolled over to rest against his shoulder. I slipped to my knees and sent up a fervent echo of the prayer I'd prayed since the accident, only this time for rest and healing for my brother in both his body and mind. When I finished, I reached for Bryson's worn Bible, sitting on top of an exquisitely bound set of Dickens, and began reading from our favorite psalms. Bryson gave a little, contented sigh, and his breathing became regular.

After quietly pushing the chairs and table up against the wall, I returned to the hallway and dragged my air mattress next to Bryson's bed. But before I lay down, I bent over my brother's ear and whispered softly enough not to wake him.

"Sweet dreams, Bryson. You're safe. I'm here."

Publisher's Cataloging-in-Publication data

Names: Thompson, Angie, author.
Title: Safe / by Angie Thompson.
Description: Lynchburg, Virginia : Quiet Waters
Press, 2019. | Summary: In the wake of a trau-
matic accident, Madison begins to suspect that
her brother's hurt goes deeper than he is willing
to show.
Identifiers: 9781951001063 (softcover) |
9781951001056 (epub)
Subjects: LCSH: Brothers and sisters–Fiction. |
Traffic accidents–Health aspects–Fiction. | Fear–
Fiction. | BISAC: FICTION / Christian / Con-
temporary.
Classification: LCC PS3620.H649 S24 2019

74020729R00020

Made in
Colum
09 Septer